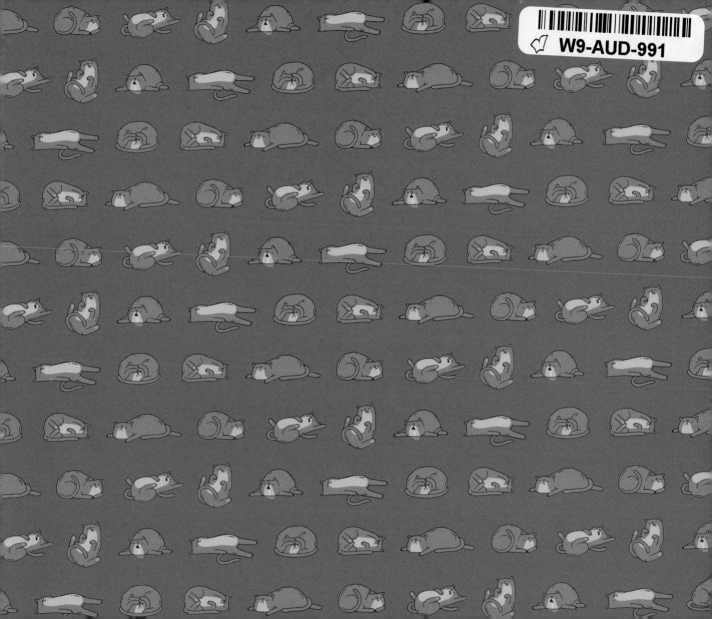

GO BACK TO SLEEP

For my dear Rudy and Sonny,
who I never *really* mind being woken up by—Zoë

For Asher and Elkie,
who bring me peaceful nights and joyful days—Mike

PENGUIN WORKSHOP
An imprint of Penguin Random House LLC, New York

First published in Australia as *Back to Sleep* by Puffin Books, an imprint of
Penguin Random House Australia Pty Ltd, 2020

First published in the United States of America by Penguin Workshop,
an imprint of Penguin Random House LLC, New York, 2021

Text copyright © 2020 by Zoë Foster Blake
Illustrations copyright © 2020 by Mike Jacobsen

Visit us online at penguinrandomhouse.com.

Library of Congress Cataloging-in-Publication Data is available.

Manufactured in China

ISBN 9780593384510   10 9 8 7 6 5 4 3 2 1

GO
BACK TO
SLEEP

BY ZOË FOSTER BLAKE • *ILLUSTRATED BY MIKE JACOBSEN*

Penguin Workshop

Finn heard a noise at his bedroom door.
His eyes flicked open in the dark.

"Come over here," Finn whispered.

Mommy walked over and stood next to his bed. "I'm *thirsty*," she said, far too loudly.

"Where's your water bottle?" Finn asked, still whispering.

"It fell down the side of my bed, and I can't reach it."

Finn sighed. "Come on, I'll get it for you."

Finn threw his legs over the edge of his bed and plopped down to the carpet.

Walking carefully so as not to tread on the enormous space station he'd built, he took Mommy by the hand and back to her room.

"Come on, go back to sleep," he said as Mommy climbed into bed and pulled up the covers. Finn reached down and grabbed her water bottle from the floor.

Mommy snatched it from him and gulped greedily. "Ahhhhhhh," she said noisily. "That's better." She flopped back down onto her pillow, grinning and wiping her mouth.

"You've got a big day at work tomorrow," said Finn. "Go to sleep."
He kissed her on the forehead before heading back to his room.

Finn had just fallen back to sleep
when he heard a voice next to his bed.
"I had a bad dream."

Daddy was standing in his undies,
peering down at Finn's face.

"Oh, buddy, I'm sorry." Finn sat up and
pulled Daddy in for a hug.

"Can I sleep with you?" said Daddy.

"Come on then, jump in," said Finn,
wiggling over as far as he could
to make room for Daddy.

Daddy climbed in and lay down, before
bolting back up. "I forgot my phone!"

"You don't need it in bed," said Finn,
eyes feeling heavy.

"ARRRRGH!" Daddy cried as he stepped on a certain space station.

"*Shhhh*, you'll wake Clem!" hissed Finn. He looked anxiously over at his baby sister's crib before leaping out of bed, grabbing Daddy's hand, and leading him into the hallway.

"BUT MY FOOT HURTS!" Daddy wailed.

"Shhhh," Finn hushed. "You'll be okay. We don't wanna wake Clem, do we? You know what happens when she wakes up."

Daddy sniffled. "You don't even care about my foot."

Finn wiped a tear from Daddy's cheek. "Course I do. Now, how about I take you back to bed so you can warm up? That sound good?"

"Can you carry me?" said Daddy.

"You're getting a bit big for that now, buddy. Come on, back to your room."

"Please?" said Daddy.

Finn sighed. "Okay. Come on."

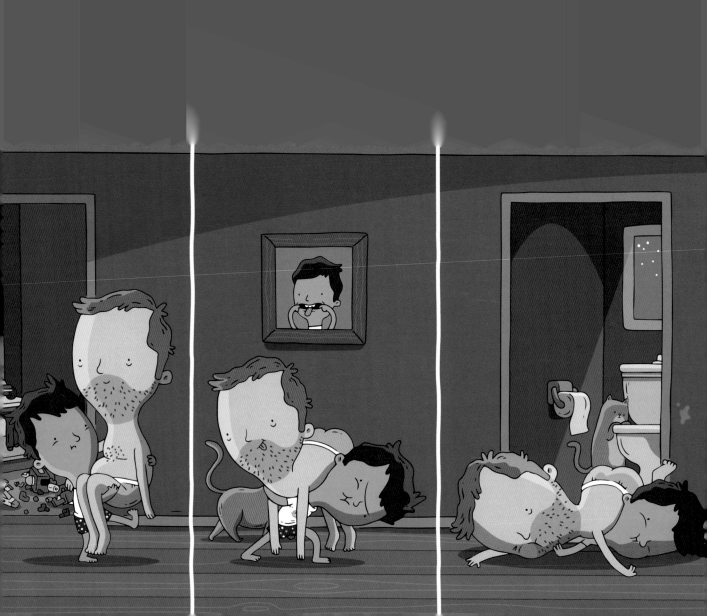

Daddy hobbled over to his side of the bed, snatched his phone, and dived under the covers.

Finn shuffled in beside him as best he could.

"Mom's taking all the covers," whined Daddy, yanking it off her.

"Hey! Wait! Let me do it," said Finn, spreading it across them evenly.

Finn felt Daddy's breathing even out
and began to carefully sneak away.

"Can you please scratch my back?" Daddy
whispered, just as Finn reached the door.

"For goodness' sake!" said Finn. "Go back to sleep."

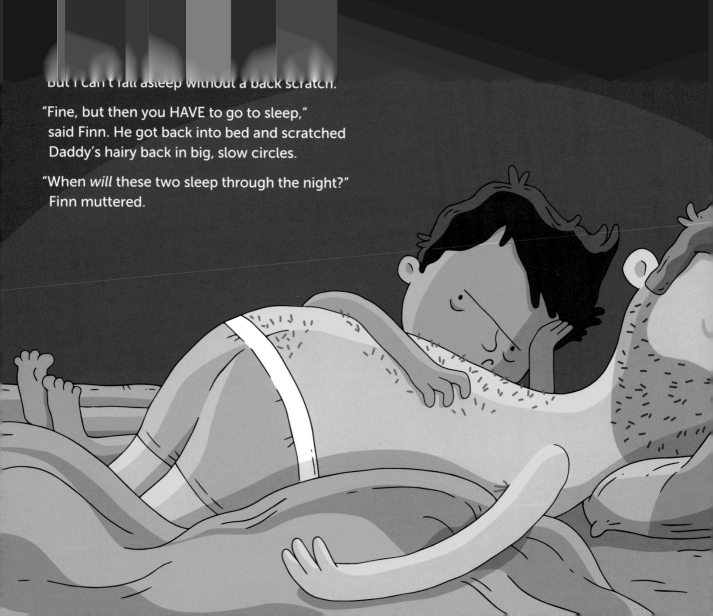

But I can't fall asleep without a back scratch.

"Fine, but then you HAVE to go to sleep,"
said Finn. He got back into bed and scratched
Daddy's hairy back in big, slow circles.

"When *will* these two sleep through the night?"
Finn muttered.

When his parents were both *finally* asleep,
Finn padded back to his room, trying not to think
about his broken space station.

He fell into bed and straight to sleep.

In what felt like five seconds' time,
someone was at his bedside.

"My bed is all wet," sobbed Mommy.
"And so are my jammies."

"Come here. It's okay. Let's clean you up," said Finn,
giving her a kiss on the forehead.

I never should have let her keep that water bottle in bed! he thought.

They walked back to Mom and Dad's bedroom. Finn got Mommy some fresh pj's and laid out a sleeping bag on her side of the bed.

"Here, jump in. It'll be fun . . . like you're a caterpillar," said Finn, half asleep.

"I don't *want* to. I want my *sheets*," said Mommy.

"Shhhh! I just got Daddy back to sleep. I don't want him waking up. In. *Now*. Off you go. BACK TO SLEEP."

Mommy huffed and reluctantly got into
the sleeping bag. Finn zipped her up.

"Can you lie with me till I fall asleep?" she said.

Finn took a deep breath.
He could never say no to that. She wouldn't be forty forever.
He needed to make the most of these precious years.

"Scoot over," he said, doing his best to fit
in the three inches left on the bed.

Later, Finn woke up, cold and confused, and shuffled back to his room. He crept in quietly, careful not to wake Clem, and curled up in his own cozy bed. Ahh, finally, back to sleep.

He closed his eyes, ignoring the light creeping in under the blind,
signaling breakfast, school, and many hours of being *un*asleep.

Just one hour of sleep, that's all he needed.

A snuffle came from the crib.

Then a thump.

A whimper.

Zoë Foster Blake is the author of this book, *No One Likes a Fart*, and also *No One Likes a Burp*. She is the mother to a boy and a girl, who she never wakes in the middle of the night for a drink or a cuddle even though it would probably be a real hoot.

Mike Jacobsen had his first exhibition at the age of three, when he drew a powerfully expressive portrait on the wall above his parents' bed. His parents remarked that it left an indelible impression upon them. And the wall. He's been drawing ever since, for clients such as Disney, Apple, the *Guardian*, 20th Century Studios, and Lonely Planet, always adding a dash of humor whenever he can.

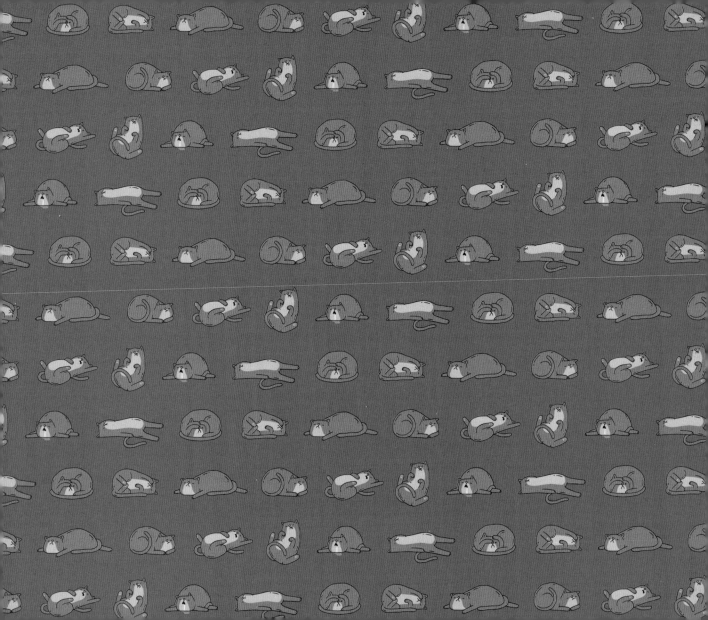